PSYCHO NIGHTMARE FREAKOUT

Copyright © 2024 by the individual authors
Designed by Ira Rat

This is a work of fiction. Names, characters, businesses, places, events, locales, and incidents are either the products of the author's imagination or used in a fictitious manner. Any resemblance to actual persons, living or dead, or actual events is purely coincidental.

This book may not be reproduced in whole or in part, except for the inclusion of brief quotations in a review, without permission in writing from the author or publisher. No part of this publication may be reproduced, stored in or introduced into retrieval system, or transmitted, in any form, or by any means (electronic, mechanical, photocopying, recording, or otherwise), without prior permission of the publisher.

Requests for permission should be directed to filthylootpress@gmail.com

EUCHARIST **RICHARD**...05
A USED CONDOM CAN BE A
HOLY RELIC TOO **GARCIA**...25
MALL GOTHS GO TO
HEAVEN **MITCHELL**...49
OUT OF HAND **STEFFENS**...80

filthyloot.com

EUCHARIST
SAM RICHARD

"So she fucking threw it out, man. And I don't mean like she just tossed it in a garbage can. She ran to the backyard and chucked the thing into the fucking creek, a dead serious look on her face. It was fucking amazing.

"I waited until she passed out, grabbed a flashlight, and went hunting for it. Thing was sitting half in the water covered in mud. Took me like an hour to find the fucker. I pushed it all the way in, just to make sure it was soaked, and hid it in the garage. After she got up in the morning, I snuck into her room and set it on her bedside table. Man, you shoulda heard the screams.

"Woman was on a fucking rampage. Tore shit through the house, out the back door and into the creek again. Screaming about Satan and praying frantically. I was dying." Todd coughed out a strangely long laugh before taking a brief pull from his cigarette. Lucky Strike, just like his dad had smoked when he was alive. He ashed into an empty Lone Star bottle, peeling the label a bit with a lazy move of his thumbnail, before continuing his story. All the others stared at him blankly, stoned and buzzed and bored in a way they couldn't quite describe if you pressed a gun to their heads.

"So I saved that shit. Put it in the garage. Figured it'd come in handy another time, maybe good for another laugh or six. Problem is I forgot about it for months until I was digging around in there yesterday, still looking for the old man's liquor stash, which might as well be ancient treasure or something. Anyhow, found the book and I pulled it out and… you guys aren't gonna fucking believe this."

A damp, filthy stench filled the room as he unzipped his backpack and pulled out a worn trash bag. It only grew worse once he revealed the contents inside: a copy of Philip Charles Rodger's *The Summoner*, covered in slimy mold and white-blue mushrooms.

For the first time since he sat down and started talking at them, Todd had the whole room's attention.

*

The devil is in your home right now. Snuck his way in through your child's toys, and cartoons. Through the music and movies and television programs your teenagers are listening to and watching. Through the games they're playing. Through th–

Stephanie crept down the narrow hallway into the living room. Her mom was passed out on the pullout couch, as expected. The tv blasting at full volume. Before her mom had a chance to hear her and wake up, she was in her tiny bedroom, door closed with a near-silent click.

She breathed a sigh of relief on the other side of the thin wooden door. Televangelist still audible as was the coughing of their apartment neighbor above, but nothing that her discman couldn't overpower. She grabbed a stack of her meager cd collection and flipped through them, trying to feel out what kind of mood she was in. She couldn't decide between Snapcase and AFI's latest–both shoplifted from Hot Topic over the past month–before she settled on *Shut Your Mouth and Open Your Eyes*. Pick-slides followed by a short, heavy riff preceded the melodic punk attack she'd been needing. The back and forth of vocals, guitars, vocals, guitars, and then a vocal call and response brought down the tension she was carrying in her shoulders.

It'd been a long fucking day.

She scream-sung along as quietly as she could, letting the music propel her forward: past high-school, past mean girls and shitty boys, past enforced class participation and homework, past her issues with her mom's insistence on both being completely detached and also amazingly overbearing; past the string of men let into the house with leering eyes. Past her friends—who she genuinely loved but were always pulling her into trouble, or worse. Past her panic attacks and grief. Past the emptiness left in her life after her dad died.

Killed himself. She forced herself to mouth the words quietly, before letting the numb pass over for a moment.

Stephanie just wanted relief and peace and freedom and fun. Maybe someone to connect with. Maybe an artist collective to be a part of while living in a shitty tiny apartment of her own that she'd barely be able to afford, but it would be all hers. And no one could take it from her.

Sitting on her rickety bed, she pulled out a notepad and a few microns—her weapon of choice—and started scribbling. No aim in particular, no goal.

Just the freedom of a blank page and a perfect pen. Her mind wandered as she drew. Thoughts of what Todd had showed them. Of his big plan. Of the group's excitement but her panic. She hated feeling like she'd dragged them all down, like she'd ruined the day. Like she was a wet-blanket, which she'd been accused of enough times that she wondered why they let her stick around.

Then again, she'd been right before. Too many dumb pranks and stunts and hair-brained ideas turning into running from the cops or fist-fights with mall-goths or fender-benders or–in one instance–two broken arms. And she'd warned them. Every single time.

So maybe she had a purpose, or at least she hoped. One of keeping them on-track if only on the occasion they listen to her, in the name of saving them all from groundings, detention, expulsion, jail, or worse. Like she was their barometer.

If only they'd listen ...

Her thoughts returned to the page, as her hand made a few final shading lines. She stared at a rough drawing of *The Summoner*, covered in slime and mushrooms; spores floating around it.

Cold dripped in her stomach and she slammed

the sketchbook closed, tossing it to the other side of the bed. Fresh anxiety grew inside her as "Triple Zero" closed out the cd, the decay of cymbals ringing out in her ears as she closed her eyes and was pulled in all directions.

*

Driving home Converge's "The High Cost of Playing God" was blasting so loud that Sean couldn't think. He reached across the center console, between Jill and Todd, to turn it down.

"Fuck man, I can't hear a goddamn thing. It's always so fucking loud back here..." He trailed off with no reaction from the pair. Todd's shitbox old Toyota was a mess. Empty soda bottles and cans, crumpled sandwich and burger wrappers, even an old, mildew-heavy towel was in the back seat, courteously of the time Todd forgot to roll his window up and it stormed overnight.

Sean shifted amongst the rubble, pushing his head closer to the front of the car, straining to hear Jill.

"...s we're gonna get sick or worse. You guys never fucking listen. If Stephanie was here she'd back me up. Honestly I'm surprised Sean is going along with this." She glared at him through the visor mirror. "Something bad is gonna happen. I can feel it."

"Fuck. Guys, I can barely fucking hear you…"

"You posers can do whatever you want. No one is forcing you. I'm doing this and I think you should too, but it's not like there's a goddamn gun to your heads." Todd said, loud enough for Sean to hear. "It's like everyone is so worried about the future but none of you are aware of how fucked the present is. I don't know what it is about this year, but y'all have been brainwashed or something. You guys used to be fun. Fucking remember that? How'd you all get so fucking old all of a sudden. You're like a bunch of fucking posers."

Jill gave Sean another look in the mirror, this time more hurt than annoyed.

They drove in unspoken discomfort until Todd pulled up at Jill's house and she and Sean poured out of the car, a trail of litter following their feet to the blacktop.

Todd didn't say a word as he pulled away, a plume of black smoke pouring from his tailpipe. Standing in the smog, Sean and Jill they let their fingers touch. First gently, then with a solid grasp of each other.

They both knew, at least to some degree, that he was right. They were changing. They were thinking about the future; trying to imagine a life away from this shitty town and its assholes and the scant few options it provided, but maybe all that dreaming was sacrificing something else.

Their hands untangled and they looked at each other awkwardly for a moment before saying good night. Jill walked up to her house and closed the door behind her without looking back because she knew if she did, she'd kiss Sean. Sean walked away from her house once the door was closed, hoping that she might of turned around.

A familiar sensation grew in his stomach as he walked the block home. One that he'd felt on and off for her over the years, but not in ages. But now that it was awake again, he couldn't move it fully out of focus.

By the time he was at home, he'd forgotten about the fight with Todd. Hell, he'd forgotten about the book and the mushrooms and all of Todd's crazy ideas. All he could think of was the softness of her hand in his; the way her fingers gently brushed his skin.

The house was dark and empty, which was to be

expected, with his dad working another overnight at the meat-packing plant's loading docks.

Sean grabbed one of his dad's Stroh's from the empty, stinking fridge and turned on the tv. A televangelist was on, ranting and red-faced. Sean didn't hear much of what he said before he threw in his Evil Dead 2 VHS on mute, and put on Misfits American Psycho before settling into their itchy brown couch for the evening; the preacher's words *we must eliminate the sin* repeating in his ears.

The mild, yellow beer was sweet and cool and calmed him, but just enough to still the quiver in his heart. For the first time in a long time he was happy. But the movie reminded him of the book. The fucking disgusting, rotting book, and he slammed the beer as quickly as he could, hoping for it to numb the dueling emotions rising in his chest.

*

"I snapped off a small handful of the mushrooms for us to try," Todd said, patting his jacket pocket. "But what I really want to do is put this thing in the HVAC system. Figure since it's just starting to get warmer again, if we can somehow make sure this fucker stays nice and damp it'll spread its spores all over the fucking school. Maybe get it shut down for a while or something."

The group stared at him, then at each other.

Jill spoke first. "Okay, but that's fucking disgusting. You shouldn't have that toxic event in your backpack, much less in Tim's room, and definitely not at fucking school. Do you even know what kind of fungus that is, Todd? And you not only want to spread it but you want us to eat that shit? Dude, you could die. We could all die just having that in here…"

She trailed off as the others joined in with questions, concerns, and excitement.

"You know I'm in, man," Tim declared, not wanting to look like a pussy. He grabbed the book from Todd's grasp, brown-green fluid squelching between his fingers and dripping onto the worn and dirty rug below.

At the smell the rest of the group shot up and scattered to the far sides of the room.

"The fuck dude, that shit is foul," Stephanie said, pulling the door open and spilling out into the hallway, assorted punk flyers rustling in her wake.

The smell followed and panic welled inside. It

wasn't right. They could all be dead already. *Fuck fuck fuck fuck* she repeated to herself silently. *Breathe. Okay, just breathe.* It had been a few months since the last panic attack, she had thought herself mostly past them. But she also knew that grief and PTSD didn't work like that. You don't just get over it, and stranger and stranger things can trigger it.

Multiple tiers of thoughts came, some louder than others, but even the quiet ones had impact. The way the carpeted floor felt beneath her feet. The cries of her mother repeating over and over and over in her ear. The smell of death when they finally found her father's body after not knowing where he was or if he was alive for weeks. The taste of something sweet and strange in her throat. The memory of riding in the passenger seat of her dad's car as a kid, singing silly songs with him and laughing. They all fought for attention.

She stared at her feet, and then her hands, trying to quell the shaking, before two sets of arms wrapped around her, comforting her.

Jill and Sean held her as she trembled and cried, trying to steady her breathing. The room behind her went quiet, but for the mild chattering of Todd and Tim, unsure of what to do; always unsure of how to help her in their awkwardness.

Eventually she calmed enough to walk home. There were offers to drive, to go with her, but she said she'd rather be alone. The raw nerve wasn't settled, but had grown over with a bit of frustration–both at herself and at Todd.

If it wasn't for me, they'd all end up killing themselves on accident she thought, walking out the front door of Tim's single-floor rambler. Dead car in the driveway. Dead skunk in the road. Dead dad. Drunk mom. Dumb friends. A few tears threatened to break from her eyelids, but she refused them.

*

Jill's heart was racing when she closed the door. She let herself breathe for a moment before carefully peeking out the small window to see if Sean was still standing there. Fortunately he had started his walk home, and she could uncoil her guts.

Her mom shouted from the kitchen, asking if she wanted any Hamburger-Helper, but she didn't answer, making a beeline to her bedroom and closing that door, too.

She immediately put on her stereo. The firing

shots of Deftones "My Own Summer" filled her small room and she wondered if the others would call her a poser for still listening to them. Much like Portishead and Nine Inch Nails, Deftones had stuck around in her transition from mall-goth to hardcore kid. They'd probably make fun of her, but she didn't care. Or really only cared enough to not tell them, but not enough to stop liking what she liked.

What's more punk than that? She asked herself before her mind returned to Sean.

What the hell were you thinking?

Their history was complicated, and it wasn't like she didn't like him, she just didn't like him as much as she liked Stephanie. But it was so nice to search for and be met with a small amount of comfort in that moment outside Todd's car. That it was a mistake was crawling down her spine.

Grabbing her backpack, she opened her English homework, hoping for a distraction, but none could be found. She'd already read Camus' *The Stranger*, and while the thought of a re-read didn't sound so bad, she couldn't focus on anything but Sean. And Todd. And the fucking moldy book.

And Stephanie. God. Poor Stephanie.

Eventually she slammed the books closed and

headed to the kitchen for something to eat. To her surprise, her mom was still in there, sitting at the kitchen table, watching a televangelist on the small black and white tv.

—fects them with poor attitudes and a lack of manners. The fabric of society is being torn apart and our children aren't even able to pray in schools any longer. We, as God-fearing parents need to stand our ground and protect our children from Satan's treacherous path. We need to protect them from themsel—

"Oh I didn't see you there.." her mom trailed off, glassy sheen over her eyes. "There's…there's food on the stovetop, if you're hungry." A zombified lilt in her voice as she kept her focus on the tv.

"Thanks mom, but I can't eat that. You know, vegetarian and all." Jill let the words hang in the air like a disappointed question. Her mom didn't respond.

Luckily there was plenty of bread and peanut-butter. She made herself a sandwich with some veggies on the side and was headed back to her room when her mom spoke again. "Was that Sean outside?" Her voice was distant. "He was always so nice. You should keep him around…"

Jill turned and looked at her. The distant,

shimmering eyes of her mother replaced by a hard and icy stare.

–ey're luring our children into sexual deviance, drug use, perversion of every sort. Satan stalks the earth like a hungry lion, seeking those he can devour, and believe me when I say that the youth of this country are the most delicious of all prey. Only in God's holy name are we able to fig–

Without a word, Jill turned back down the hall and into her room, fire growing in her chest.

*

"Like I told those guys, none of you have to do this with me if you don't want to." Todd spoke softly, with an air of compassion and understanding that hadn't been there before. "I'm gonna do it, and I'd rather not do it alone, but it's your choice." He held a small pile of dry white-blue mushrooms that had started to yellow at the edges in the palm of his hand.

The Nerve Agents "Unblossomed" played low on the stereo.

Tim was the first to take one. He didn't hesitate before putting it in his mouth with an *Eww* and chewing it quickly. "Man," Sean laughed, "You guys remember when we were all straight edge, like last year?"

The group laughed in an uneasy chorus that quickly grew full and earnest.

"Fuck it." Sean grabbed one, popping it into his mouth. "That was around the same time you two got into a fight with those fucking mall posers. I think we all broke edge that same fucking weekend."

"Oh man, I got in so much trouble when I showed up at home, drunk." Tim coughed out a laugh, still chewing.

"That's the fucking spirit, let's go!" Todd said, eating one. "Poser fuckers deserved that shit, too. Buncha goddamn shitheads."

Stephanie hated watching them do this. But she also hated how the other night went; how outside of the group she so suddenly felt. Outside of a group of people that had understood her more than anyone else in her life ever had. Outside of a group of people who had been there for her when her life was at its worst, and had continued to show up for her when times were tough.

She tamped down the panic that wanted to come. Silenced the voices telling her that this would all go horribly wrong; that they—she—couldn't handle this and it would all end in disaster. With a will of cold detachment, she grabbed a mushroom, holding it in her fingers for a moment—which brought subtle memories of seeing her father's body that she pushed from her mind—before shoving it into her mouth, chewing the fetid tasting fungus as little as she could, and choking it down. She wasn't sure who was more surprised, her or the group.

"Well fuck, I'm not gonna be the only one. If the most cautious and wise amongst us is down to party, then I guess I am too." Jill swallowed hers in one gulp just as Tim turned the stereo up louder and the drums in "Level 4 Outbreak" kicked on.

A frenzy punched through them. One beyond a weekend free from school and the bullshit of other kids, one laced with group mania as they anxiously awaited the mushrooms to drop. It didn't take very long.

Tim got hit first, like something crawled up his leg and slithered through his spine. A primordial taste in the back of his throat, one of acidic metal but experienced before any human understanding metal existed—an ancient sensation. He was being pulled to back and to the left, like chains were hooked into him. He hadn't anticipated his equilibrium getting so fucked, but he cackled all the way to where the wall and the floor met. His head put a dent in the drywall with a soft thud and the rest of the group laughed.

Then Stephanie, a spider's itch in her lungs, like something was taking root. Not in a coughing or concerning way, at least not that she could tell. She felt like she was only two-inches but also twenty-feet tall all at once. The sensation also sent her to the floor, in a more graceful, yet still awkward collapse to her knees.

Staring at the carpet she noticed every single fiber of every single thread, or every single thread of every single fiber; she didn't remember which was right, which made her laugh. But something was different about the rug. Not in the swimming and shifting patterns, though those were also present like the intermingling and detaching of a thousand illegible metal logos. No. There were small, lumpy growths. They were discolored, much lighter than the dark browns and burnt oranges native to the rug.

And the longer she studied them, the more they grew. Not by inches or even centimeters, but in microscopic increments that only she could discern. Tiny sprouts from each strange pore until they had built a new layer and a new layer and a new layer until she was repeating those words over and over out loud.

No one was paying attention. Todd was speaking, but his words sounded backmasked or from an alien tongue. His eyes glowed in a diffused, matte way, but only in fleeting moments. Another thing no one else noticed.

Sean tried to talk with Todd. A desperate need for clarification surged through him, but Todd's gibberish only got less comprehensible. What had sounded like cut-up bits of words devolved into atonal grunts and shrieks.

A cold fell onto the room, sinking into everyone's guts.

Jill shivered and cried out, coughing violently until flecks of dark-red littered the wall and carpet. When she could breathe again, she watched small sprouts blossom from the specks. She ran fingers across her mouth, smearing the blood. Soft stubble met her fingertips.

Tim stopped laughing long enough to vomit into his hamper. What didn't make it floated in the air like bubbles. They were soft and gentle looking, like a taraxacum seedhead. One hit the wall and silently erupted, painting the corner of the room in pale-green mold.

"Oh what the fuck!?" he managed to say before his eyes rolled into the back of his skull and he hit the ground again, fuzzy green growing on his lips; dense mold sprouting from between the fingers on his right hand. They pulsed like they were crawling as they bloomed out.

In quick succession, each of them were pulled to the ground, coughing, vomiting, and crying slime, mold, and giant spores. Only Todd stood, babbling his own secret language. Either unaware or uncaring of what was happening to the rest of the group.

For the first time in a long time he felt whole inside. Confident and secure. All his thoughts poured out of his lips like there was no barrier between his brain and his mouth. And then, thoughts that maybe weren't his; like there was no barrier between the universe and his mouth. He breathed in through the crown of his head and his fingertips, just under the nails. The sensation tickled.

He remembered some of these sensations from trying psilocybin mushrooms in the fall, but this was on another level. He loosened himself and eased into it, letting it take him wherever it flowed. No anxiety or care. He trusted the process. He trusted himself. He trusted the universe.

It cracked open inside him, like an egg. Yolk and white dripping down the inside of his chest. A sensation both in body and in soul. The merging of the logos and the flesh. There was no him and no other, there was no delineation between what made him and what made the universe: they were all one organism. One breathing, laughing, crying, fucking, dying, living, consuming, sleeping, hunting, nourishing, rotting, pondering thing.

The universe led him out of the room—book in hand like a sacred text that must be shared with the world—out of the house, into his car, and to the school. It was time to spread this hidden knowledge.

The Toyota enveloped him like the ocean, hugging him tightly with warmth and pleasant machine-noise. Todd thought about his body as a machine being driven the way he was driving the car; the mushrooms flowing through him taking some special seat inside and putting him into gear.

Shimmering lines glowed on the ground and in orbs above. Everything moving both in slow-motion and sped up; like when a camera zooms in while pulling back. This off-kilter sensation. It itched in his veins and he breathed in the universe through his fingernails to ground him.

A man was ranting on the radio and instead of turning it off, Todd just laughed until there was nothing in his mind but laughter; until his laughter turned alien and strange and full of the alien and strange laughter of his friends. Disembodied. The car floated on its own, stopping perfectly at the back of the school.

His ears were warm with fuzz as he exited the running car, approached the building, and kicked in a basement window to the HVAC room. The school had updated to a modern, efficient model the prior year, finally getting rid the ancient boiler that had been warming the school since it was built in the 1920s.

The book was wet in his hand. A trail of slime behind him, heading back to the car. Patches of mold had already started to sprout. Not subtly like in Tim's room either. These were already centimeters tall, and Todd wondered how long he'd been standing there. *The seduction of our youth with drugs and perversion* repeated over and over in his ears. He wanted to laugh more, but it also reminded him of some weak-ass nu-metal sample he'd heard back when he listened to that shit.

Perversion.

Perversion.

Perversion.

Perversion.

The word was tactile on his brain as he contemplated it, fitting it into some down-tuned caveman riff he built in his head. There was an off-kilter lilt that covered him in goosebumps. Looking down again, the moldy splotches were inches tall, and pooling out like blood in snow.

He thought he forgot how the dumb riff went, but he realized it was a fan inside the HVAC system making the noise. Lost art. Forgotten genius. True creation. Made by machine. Organics forged of mechanical parts.

He opened the access panel and tried to set the book down inside it, but he couldn't let it go. It was fused to his flesh. Thin strands of white mold covered his arms like he'd walked through a thousand cobwebs. They crawled up his arm and onto his chest. The mechanical riff kept repeating in his head like true industrial music.

Perversion.

Perversion.

Perversion.

Perversion.

His mind went empty but for the pumping rhythm. All thoughts, fears, aspirations, doubts, desires, apprehensions, secrets, truths vibrated out of him and into the universe. He watched them float away in large white orbs that tore open with a quiet, wet slap when they touched the ceiling and walls and floor and other machinery. Spreading their essence; spreading his essence.

He tried to move, but his arms had dried out, turning to a billowing dust, while his core and neck grew soft and wet, expanding their reach into the access panel in bright orange tendrils and fuzzy white puffs, around the machine, around his entire body, and out the shattered window.

The line of slime that led from his car blossomed outside and in. Inside was coated in a quickly growing sickly seafoam fluff that folded over itself with repeated spores that couldn't find the lone open door, getting larger and larger until it was full, spilling out onto the blacktop below. Blooming dots on the ground outside blended into the grass, consuming it, and quickly covering the perimeter of the school. The growth multiplied, stretching in all directions.

From inside the car came a muffled *Amen*.

A USED CONDOM CAN BE A HOLY RELIC TOO

XAVIER GARCIA

When Ellie grows up she wants to travel the country and when Luis grows up he wants to be more than his father, but the only problem is that Ellie and Luis have already grown up and whatever happened to wanting more.

Luis looks at Ellie across the filth and Ellie can tell Luis is looking and she wishes so very badly she could walk over and say hi.

Neither makes a move and they continue doing what it is that they were doing: Ellie talks to Mark and Luis continues drinking and brooding like some moody fuck. The place smells awful.

When Ellie grows up she wants to live in a cozy house, a place where she feels warm and safe like on TV, and when Luis grows up he just wants to live somewhere that doesn't smell like vodka.

This place is neither.

A house on the edge of town left abandoned after the factory closed, it now looks less like a former home and more like some suburban time capsule, North American Chernobyl. Factory meltdown sans nuclear but still resulting in familial degradation. With everything left so intact you can practically see the smiling white faces that used to live there. That rotted couch against the wall large enough to have once comfortably fit an entire nuclear family on it; cuddled sweet and smiling in the soft glow of the television. Now the couch bleeds suburban radiation over yellowed linoleum floors.

But drinking here isn't new. Two years graduated and Luis and Ellie are still getting high and drunk and stupid in the same abandoned neighborhood with the same group of goths or punks or freaks or who knows what the fuck they are at least they're wasted.

Luis looks around the room and sees Ellie still talking to Mark.

Luis wonders if Ellie even cares that he's there and Ellie knows Luis is looking at her and she still very much wishes she could go over and say hi. She's looking so sexy in that black tank top that cuts off at her midriff, that long black hair making her look even more pale and sad and with those lips smeared in black Luis can't stop looking and Ellie can tell he's watching so she goes over for another beer, getting down on her haunches to dig around the bag, facing away from him and he tries not to look but with her bent so low like that in front of him and in that top her back dimples look just like sex and they never should have fucked.

Last Sunday they never should have fucked.

Friends since kids, friends through high school, and now it's all ruined.

Every time Ellie thinks about it she gets angry. Not because they slept together, but because of how weird Luis got afterwards. Friends since kids, friends through high school and not a single phone call. And she knows why. He's scared of her brother, Eddie. Scared of what he'll say if he found out. Every time Ellie thinks about it she gets angry.

Ellie stands back up and walks over to Mark, sipping her new drink as he rambles on.

Luis continues drinking and brooding like some moody fuck.

When Luis grows up he wants to be more than his father but the only problem is he grew up to be just as weak as he is and Ellie still can't believe how strong he looks. It makes her smile to think of the skinny boy he was in school, that Mexican goth kid with an accent that made him insecure and moody and quiet. A few summers working construction with his uncle and so much has changed. He's grown lean and muscular. He's shaved his head, and now Ellie looks at him sitting there, still moody, with those little crosses dangling from each ear and he looks so dangerous she could die.

But they slept together and why can't he just stop being so scared.

But that's not fair. That's just her being angry.

Because Ellie's scared too.

A door in the hallway bursts open and Eddie walks into the room, mean smile on his face.

"You guys have to see what I found in the basement," he says.

"Dude, I am *not* going in that basement," says Mark.

"Shut the fuck up, yes you are," says Eddie and that's the end of the conversation.

Ellie can't help but frown.

And it's not because Mark's such a pushover, still the same chubby punching bag from high school, self-esteem so low he takes Eddie's bullying as friendship. It's not even because Eddie is trying to boss them all around like he always does. Ellie frowns because she knows even if they don't want to, her and Luis will end up in the basement just the same as Mark.

Luis sips his warm beer.

"What's in the basement?"

"You'll see. Now get off your ass and come down here."

Luis can't help but frown.

"Fine," he says. But he wants very badly to go home. Without Ellie to talk to, these Saturdays just aren't what they used to be.

Luis wishes he were someone else as he makes his way into the hallway, Eddie still smiling as he turns towards the basement door. Hair long and dyed black like his sister, lips smeared in black like his sister, Eddie and Ellie are alike in so many ways and yet he lacks the warmth of his sister, that glow of his sister, Ellie wishes she weren't his sister as she makes her way into the hallway and suddenly wishes she were someone else.

Eddie and Mark go down first just as Luis and Ellie reach the door.

Luis stops and the two make eye contact. The

moment lingers in the gloom of the peeling hallway.

"You first," he says.

"Thanks," she says back, finally pulling her eyes from him and heading downwards.

An abandoned house within an abandoned street and the industrial death of suburbia can most strongly be felt here. Vacuous where it should feel nostalgic, every step down the flight of stairs echoes and reverbs like faraway metal clanging in an empty factory.

Luis and Ellie take a moment to adjust their eyes when they reach the bottom. Two dirty high windows the only source of light.

"What are we meant to be looking at?" asks Luis.

"There. In the back," says Eddie and his voice sounds weird.

The group make their way towards the other end of the basement and at first Luis and Ellie can't make out what it is they're looking at. Something plastered against the wall. Something large. Something doughy and pale. Something fleshy. Something that looks shaped like a person.

But then all at once it hits, that something something against the wall is the something something that it looks like. That something

something smeared against the wall, that fleshy doughy thing plastered across the wall is a man. His stretched and kneaded muscles rotting and bonding into the brick like human papier-mâché, no paper and glue, all flesh and pus, all viscous and shiny like chewed up bubble gum. Arms extended into the crucifix position like he fell backwards one day and became stuck that way.

"Oh my god, we need to call the hospital," says Ellie, her eyes wide with disgust.

No hospital.

And the voice comes from the rotted dough against the brick.

And holy shit, the man's alive.

Luis puts an arm in front of Ellie and pushes her back. Suddenly afraid of either of them catching whatever disease he has.

"Dude, we need to get you to the hospital," Luis half yells.

No hospital. I'm fine, it says as its maggot white lips turn up into a smile.

And then knowing that the smear of flesh against the wall is in fact a man they all take a better look; Eddie smiling back at it. How is this even possible? How is the man alive?

Pale mouth within an unkempt beard and Ellie wonders if the man is homeless and Luis thinks the same, but the more they look the more confused they get. His arms extended into the crucifix position, but he's also nearly naked, nothing on him but a ragged cloth across his waist and a solid disk-like headpiece that sits atop his tangled mop of hair. It looks liked faded bonze. But then there's something else, something they all missed within the doughy rot. Running down the man's abdomen is a large and open wound. Running a foot long down his navel, the gaping wound looks red and sore and curls around the edges and though the gash looks fresh, it does not bleed.

He sees them looking.

Reach in.

"What? No way," says Mark, but Eddie takes one step forward.

"Eddie, don't be an idiot," says Ellie.

"You're all a bunch of pussies," he spits and inches closer.

Reach in, my friend. A gift for you.

"Eddie, what the hell is the matter with you. Leave the guy alone. We need to call 911."

"Shut the fuck up, Luis. Don't make me hit you."

Luis frowns. He can feel Ellie watching.

And Eddie flashes them both a grin like he knows exactly what he's doing before taking off his shirt and stretching in a classic show-off move. His long, lean torso corpse-pale like his face, black hair streaming down his shoulders, and is it weird to say his smile reminds Luis of his mother. Just so mean and cruel and petty.

And Luis is about to say something else before Eddie reaches in.

Before anyone can stop him, Eddie pushes his fingers into the man's open wound, two at first, almost gentle, the man's flesh lips red and sore and spreading as Eddie slips and inches all the way down to his knuckles, and then the bloodless gash contracts, it's all too much, and begins sucking back Eddie's hand all the way down to his wrist.

And he smiles.

"Oh my god," yells Ellie.

And he smiles.

And Eddie yanks back his hand. But it's stuck.

And he smiles.

Another panicked tug and nothing. And then finally a wet popping sound as he pulls out hard, but he actually manages to do so. His hand is free. Only there's something more. He's holding something now.

Something thick.

And this time Eddie smiles for in his hand is a fat wad of cash.

No one knows what to say.

They eye each other up in complete confusion.

Fear thick in the basement gloom before Eddie tosses his head back in uncharacteristic laughter. Sweet relief across his face.

"Is that…money?" asks Luis.

"Fuck yeah, it's money," says Eddie and slaps the wad of bills against Luis's chest.

And now it's Mark that's laughing.

"My turn," he says.

"Mark, no!"

Before Mark shoves his fingers into the man's open wound, his eyes rolling back, only to pull out a three-hundred-dollar bottle of champagne.

"Toast anyone?" he asks after his hand is free. This time there was no need for yanking, the wound is worked and ready.

And a toast, ha ha very funny.

When Ellie grows up she wants to have a loving group of friends like the funny smiling people in her favourite sitcoms and when Luis grows up he wants to not wish that he were dead, but now Mark's popped the bottle and the only problem is that Ellie and Luis have already grown up and all of this is actually happening.

Mark takes a deep pull from the champagne bottle and passes it to Eddie.

"Great thinking," says Eddie and Mark is smiling huge, his moment in the sun, his moment of rare appreciation coming from the person whose appreciation matters least.

Ellie looks at Eddie, his black-lipsticked mouth pulled into a smile and she wishes she could break his face.

"What is it?" says Luis looking at the man smeared across the wall. "An angel?"

"He doesn't look like an angel. He's got no wings," says Ellie.

"Look at that thing on his head. It's like a halo. Maybe he's a saint?" says Mark.

And then Eddie smiles.

"The Patron Saint of Fucks," he says. "That's who he is. That's his name. A toast to the Patron Saint of Fucks."

And he smiles.

And Eddie chugs down a bit more of that

expensive booze and shoves the bottle into Luis's hand.

Luis frowns but takes a sip and it's the sweetest drink he's ever had. Turns out miracles taste like layers of citrus, nuts, and olive oil richness. He wipes his mouth with the back of his hand and passes the bottle over to Ellie.

They make eye contact for only just a second as she takes it from him and takes a little sip herself.

And she hates that she drank, drank from a bottle that came out the open, unbleeding wound of a rotting man's stomach. But more than that, she hates that she felt compelled to, compelled to by her brother out of fear of pushing him to meanness. But no, that's what it used to be, it used to be only meanness. And that she could live with. But like her father, meanness was never going to be enough, and lately, like her father, Eddie's words have turned to fists. And if only she could tell Luis. She hates how scared Luis is of Eddie. Almost as scared as she is of telling him. But not because she thinks Luis will judge her, he's always been so sweet, she's scared of what he'll do, because what if he does nothing? Because, what if Ellie tells Luis why she wants to leave home so badly and nothing changes.

Everything remains the same. That would leave a mark blacker than any bruise.

"A toast to the Patron Saint of Fucks," says Ellie. Tears prickling her eyes.

And he smiles.

And though the tears are not yet there, Luis can tell there's something wrong with Ellie, and goddamn he should have called. He takes the bottle from her hands and drinks.

"A toast to the Patron Saint of Fucks," he says and takes another swig.

He's not really scared of Eddie, that skinny shirtless fuck. He knows that he can take him. There's just something in his meanness, something that reminds him of his mom. And like his dad, when words turn cruel, he crumbles and grows silent, frozen and complacent, and then falls into a bottle. All his life he hated his father for his weakness, but of course he turned out to be just like him. Another sip, this one deeper, because of course he turned out to be so meek and little, Ellie must think him such a pussy.

And he hands Mark back the bottle for him to finish.

And he does.

"Another," says Eddie.

"No, I'm done. This is weird. I'm going home," Luis says, and gives Ellie a little glance. Hoping that she'll come with him, away from Eddie and away from Mark and away from the decaying saint smeared across the wall.

But then that looks flashes across Eddie's face, that look that says he's growing mad.

"You're not going anywhere. We only just got started," says Eddie.

And Luis meets his eyes. He's so sick of this.

"Let them go, Eddie. More for us," says Mark, reaching back into the Patron Saint of Fucks's red and open gash.

And talking back, that's a mistake Mark knows better not to make, but he knows he's made it the moment he feels Eddie's hateful grip clamp down around the backside of his neck.

"Don't ever tell me what to do," he growls.

Mark's hand still inside the open flesh. The bloodless wound contracting, it's all too much.

And he smiles.

"Eddie, let go of him," says Ellie.

"What did I just say? Don't tell me what to do."

And the wound, as if sensing what's to come,

stretches wider. Its edges unfurling sweetly like the red blooming of cut skin, before Eddie pushes Mark through the swollen flesh lips of the Patron Saint of Fucks's navel gash.

And Mark is gone.

Luis can feel the blood drain from his face and Ellie suddenly feels like throwing up.

"Dude. Why did you do that?" is all that it occurs to him to say.

"What?" says Eddie, smiling, almost bashful, as he pushes his hair out of his face.

"You stupid shit, who knows were Mark went."

"Go get him then, Luis. If you care so much."

And now the mood has changed. The basement no longer feeling vacuous, the metallic air electric. Eddie stares into Luis's eyes in that dare-you-to-say-something way that reminds Luis so very much of his mother.

And Ellie still feels like throwing up, who the hell knows where Mark went down that open abdomen. In a haze she wanders over to the Patron Saint of Fucks, hoping to who-knows-what, maybe get a better look, but before she's able to get too close, Eddie grabs her by the hair and tosses her back onto the floor. She falls backwards wincing, but makes no noise, she's used to staying quiet.

"Stay back Ellie, I think your boyfriend wants to join Mark. Maybe I'll help him."

And he smiles.

And again, that grin, so cruel and mean and mocking and so full of little meanings all meant to make him feel so very small. And if that was it, if it was just the meanness, Luis probably would have stomached it. But it was more than that. It was the practiced ease by which Eddie had grabbed her hair, by the plain comfortability by which pain was dealt. And all at once Luis recognizes something between Eddie and Ellie that he sees in himself and his own family. Turns out Eddie reminded Luis of his mother for a reason.

When Luis grows up he wants to be more than his father and when Ellie grows up she wants to break her brother's face and we all have to grow up sometime, Ellie grabs Eddie's hair from behind by two aggressive handfuls and pulls him down and the little bitch is screaming and so Luis walks over to the Patron Saint of Fucks and sticks his fingers into the red and open wound, two at first, almost gentle, until he pushes in his hand all the way to his wrist.

"You know what your problem is, Eddie," says

Luis.

Eddie on the ground, doing his best to protect his face from Ellie's kicks, but he manages to turn his head and make eye contact.

"You've never really gotten to see how weak you are."

And then Luis pulls with all his might, flesh lips spreading impossibly wide, until he manages to pull out that thing that he had wished for. Ellie turns to look and at first can't make out what it is. It's something large, something pale, something fleshy. And then she bursts out into laughter when she realizes what that something something is.

Because that pale and fleshy thing that Luis pulls out of the Patron Saint of Fucks's open abdomen is another Eddie. And false-Eddie, just like the real one on the ground, looks scared as shit.

"Look Eddie, look how weak you are."

And Luis brings down his fist onto false-Eddie's corpsewhite face, blood and teeth spilling out onto the basement floor.

"I mean it, Eddie. Look. This is how weak you are."

Luis climbs on top false-Eddie, throwing down heavy fist after heavy fist and Ellie looks across the room at Luis making pulp out of her false-brother's face and she can't believe how strong he looks and with those little crosses dangling from his ears, he looks so dangerous she could die and Luis look over just in time to see Ellie smashing the champagne bottle over the real Eddie's head before crawling on top of him, and he tries not to look but with her bent so low like that and in that top her back dimples look just like sex and then she looks over her shoulders once again but this time they make eye contact and he's so very sorry for never calling and she wishes so very badly she could go over and say hi.

They turn back and deliver even more blows to their respective Eddies, again and again until their arms hurt, and even then, they keep on going because this feels only right. Because let this be the death of radiation-choked suburbia, let this be the meltdown of nuclear familial homes, let this be a final toast to the Patron Saint of Fucks, because there's really nothing else to say than our father who art passed out at home, suck a dick, die slow.

When they finish, Ellie and Luis are exhausted.

Without saying a word, they help one another pile both Eddies into the Patron Saint of Fuck's red and open wound.

One, then two. Down goes real Eddie.

And he smiles.

And then Ellie and Luis find themselves alone, facing one another in front of a rotting saint looking down on them like a wedding officiator.

Under its bronze halo, the smeared saint is smiling.

Luis looks into Ellie's eyes.

Black mascara all runny down her freckles and mixing with her brother's blood.

"I should have called."

"Duh."

And they laugh.

And then Ellie decides to take a chance, unsure of what Luis will do.

But she reaches down into the smeared saint's open abdomen, almost gentle, and pulls out two train tickets to Montreal.

Luis looks down at the tickets and smiles. There's nothing he'd love more.

He nods over at the wad of cash on the basement floor and Ellie smiles huge and nods.

Luis turns to pick it up and then stops. Instead, reaching into the smeared saint's open wound for a second wad of cash.

"Just in case."

She laughs. And it's the sweetest sound he's ever heard.

Luis and Ellie can't wait to finally grow up.

MALL GOTHS GO TO HEAVEN
MATTHEW MITCHELL

Colin made it to The Ditch before any of his friends. It was hot outside, so he scored a lift from his Mom. He made her drop him off at Sonic, then skated a quarter mile to the slab of concrete behind the Mall. It was a quick ride over, but already his skeletal pits were damp beneath his trench coat.

The trench was a black leather duster, two sizes too big, and was purchased by his Grandpa at an Australian themed steakhouse. After the old man died, Colin was sad for a long time. His Mom found the coat in a closet last summer and gave it to him. Once he put it on, it never really came off.

Colin rode his skateboard up and down the gentle, cement slope as he waited for his friends. He made a concerted effort to take it slow, to not get too sweaty. If his deodorant wore off before the girls got there, *before they took him into the changing room*, maybe they would call the whole thing off. They might decide not to make out with him if he stunk. The girls would make up new nicknames—meaner ones. The halls at school would echo with insults. They would all laugh at him.

Colin slicked back his rat-blonde mullet with a greasy palm. He kicked back on his skateboard, caught it awkwardly, and decided he should cool off before the others arrived. The grass on either side of The Ditch was sparse, divided by mud, so he plopped his baggy denim seat onto the concrete; chunky skate shoes propped on his griptape-covered deck. Colin pulled a headset over his ears, slid his hand into a cavernous pant pocket, and fumbled around blindly. His fingers found the triangular 'Play' button on his Walkman and pushed it.

A bonesaw guitar riff poured into his brain. Screeching howls of incestual desire and creeping vines of thorn. Blast beats and staccato snares. His favorite band. The good shit. Not like all the posers on MTV. This was real. *Raw*.

Palms to skull, he lay back on the cement and shut his eyes. Languid, he dreamed of haunted castles and gothic longing. Aimless visions of ruby, dripping lips. Flashing scripture in clove smoke ghosts and velvet beds. Colin saw Cara and Andrea painted in psychedelic blacklight hues. Dancing, waving, they beckoned him...

Something heavy pushed against his chest. Colin thrashed and opened his eyes.

A brown waffle-stomper boot pinned him by the sternum. Up the JNCO piped leg, Tony stared down at him with a sharp-toothed grin. His eyes were black and glassy like a possum; the mark of his beast, a signifier that he was a teen hellbent on ignorant destruction and fiendish violence. Tony carried eyes that truly terrified when met with the rational; unblinking and insane.

Lucky bastard, Colin thought in his jealousy, and not for the first time.

"Morning, *Colon*," Tony said. His hair was spiked with bright blue gel and he sported his usual XXL Slipknot t-shirt; a mainstay he proudly earned by chucking balls at the county fair.

"Get the fuck—" Colin coughed and squirmed beneath the boot "—off of me."

"Is widdle Colon weady for him big day?" Tony stomped down on his chest in rhythmic, bouncing steps that pushed the wind from Colin's gut. "*Oh*," Tony cried, high and girlish. "Give it to me, Cawa.

Uhhh…Stwoke my widdle peepee, Andwea!"

I'll fucking kill you, Colin tried to shout, but found he could not. Tiny gusts of his voice whimpered out as Tony jogged the boot up and down: "You–umb– mother–er–I– fuh– hate…"

"Alright, Tony, that's enough," a voice said, muffled as if from beneath a fathomless lake; a voice beyond the black spots at the corners of his vision—a blackness that threatened to swallow everything. "He's gonna pass out, dude. Let him up."

"Shit, okay." Tony pulled back his leg reluctantly and released him.

Colin choked on fresh wind. He rubbed at his chest, sputtered various croaking curses.

"Shut up, pussy," Tony said. "You're fine."

"Yeah, don't be a bitch."

A sturdy, pale arm reached down and clutched his trenchcoat by the collar. Colin was hauled up into the face of Brandon who glared at him with perverse fascination.

Brandon was lithe where Tony was husky. Colin was emaciated where Brandon was trim. A Golden God, draped in black. Acne scars and chiseled features. Corpse-white hair in a dense widow's peak. The quintessential backyard wrestling hellraiser every suburban neighborhood fears to call its own.

"It's your big day, *Colon*," Brandon said. "Can't have you blacking out before the fun starts."

Tony snickered. His sharkish teeth clicked as he laughed. "Yeah," he said, "but after..."

"After the girls have him, you two can buttfuck a hole to China for all I care," Brandon snapped. "But until then, we got to keep our Colon clean, don't we?"

"Fuck yeah, you do. Hands off, boys."

Startled by the familiar command, the three boys turned. Nostrils flared. Pupils widened. Brandon let go of Colin's duster and backed away sheepishly.

Two girls stalked across the muddy field towards them: Cara in her leather bell bottoms, garish orange flames stitched from the hems to lick her knees. Andrea in fishnet sleeves, tight bondage pants with black canvas straps and endless loops of cheap aluminum chains. The girls wore matching rubber Frankenstein boots with six inch soles; swirls of darksome glitter and midnight purple shadows painted across both pairs of eyes.

"Hope you washed your balls today, *Colon*," Cara cackled.

"Fuck, dude," Andrea clapped a ring laden hand across Cara's painted lips. "He's gonna hear you..."

A turquoise El Camino—Cara's Dad's—drifted lazily along the curb behind them.

"I don't give a shit what he hears," Cara said. She shoved Andrea's hand away, swatted the shorter girl's rear in a jangle of chains. Cara began to moan and gag. She wound her long two-tone hair into her fist— jerked her own neck back and forth, puckered her drooling mouth, crossed her eyes.

Tony, Brandon, Andrea, all of them cried with joy at her daring display. They slapped knees and stomped their boots. Colin was quiet.

Though the El Camino was several yards away, he could feel the radiation of a fatherly gaze, could see the glowing pupils watching he and the other boys from behind the wheel, searching their intentions, searing them with fatherly judgment. Sniffing the air for dogs.

Cara turned and gave a sparkling wave to the El Camino with a trickle of spit still dangling from her bottom lip. "Bye-bye, *Daddy*," she hollered, cocked her hip.

To Colin's relief, the car picked up speed, rounded into a cul-de-sac, and was gone.

The girls clambered down into The Ditch in a flurry of laughter. Cara waltzed over to Brandon and Tony, draped her long, scarred arms across their necks.

"You're fucked up," Brandon told her.

"You ain't seen shit," she replied.

Andrea slithered behind Colin's back and hopped onto his skateboard. She grabbed him by the shoulders to keep steady. Lips pressed to the side of his beet-red ear, she whispered: "Ready for this?"

Colin went stiff in the pants, thanked God for the extra wide cut of his jeans. He nodded. "Yeah."

"Let's go," Andrea said, and took him by the hand.

*

The Mall was quiet that morning. Just a few early shoppers, the usual groups of classmates killing boredom on the last leg of summer vacation, a handful of elderly walkers still milling about after their pre-dawn jaunt across tiled floors of the jagged monolith.

Jeb Jacobs, the town drunk turned born-again nuisance, ambled alone with his typical stack of hand printed Chick tracts and a filthy "God Hates You" tee. He muttered quick judgments at the black clothed kids he passed. Stuck his finger in their faces.

Colin paid the babbling zealot no mind. He moved slowly through the beige halls like bait being trolled down beneath rolling waves; the same waters he felt so near to hand when Tony had nearly squeezed the life from behind his eyes. Deep, heavy footfalls. A death march towards his birth as an "I kissed two chicks" non-loser.

He stared at Cara's behind, at the way it swayed from side to side.

Andrea clasped one of her chains to the useless hammer-loop stitched below his pocket. She twisted the links around her plump fingers, and gave him a tug when he began to fall behind.

I hope this is real, he thought. *I hope this is happening.*

Brandon watched Colin with a subtle smile. It was a hateful, knowing thing.

As the group passed the World of Wonders shop, Tony cast his yearning gaze at an enormous sword mounted on the back wall. He salivated for the dark red handle of cheaply dyed wood, the knuckle-binding fist brace along its outer rim; fawned over its useless, serrated edges that no sane blacksmith would forge—the desperate, swooping blade.

For years, the dark eyed boy felt as if the sword called to him, that he could hear it speak his name. Tony knew that one day he would pull it from its hooks to wield it with wild abandon throughout the Mall. He wanted to chop at random, flailing limbs—would jam the blade down helpless, screaming throats—could taste bloody slaughter in the rheumy depths of his mind.

One of these days, Tony thought.

Cara and Andrea drifted in a realm of their own. They flashed teeth at men in polos, touched their hair, and held hands. No game existed which they had not played; all things known, every moment understood.

The kids at last came upon a bright, buzzing sign that read *BAZOOKAS* in slippery ropes of rainbow neon. They stopped in front of the store and Brandon waved. A pudgy, older guy behind the checkout desk returned the gesture. He wore dual lip rings and an ill-fitting flatbill cap. Brandon and Tony walked up to the counter. They flipped out their palms to catch high-fives from the fat faced employee.

Cara looked over her shoulder at Colin. She flicked her tongue and rolled her eyes behind a curtain of dark hair. Andrea pulled on his makeshift leash, lead him through the storefront.

The dark shelves on either side were filled with an assortment of sex-toys, strobe lights, and novelty t-shirts. There was a rack of weed-themed blacklight posters, a case of brightly colored piercing studs, and a wide variety of joke gifts and gags: rubber turds, bongs in the shape of turgid members, inflatable furniture, glow-in-the-dark door beads. The sort of place a kid could pick up a studded collar to match their leather gauntlets. A haven for gangster rap accoutrement and frat houseparty favors; where you could pay a legal adult man ten bucks to let you and your friends lick necks in the dressing room for a half hour.

Colin was aware of this economic microcosm, but always assumed it was a system far above his weight class. Stuff for the popular kids. Pastime dalliances of attractive druggies and all-star ball players. Yet there he was, watching Tony and Brandon—the most frightening, and therefore *coolest*, kids he knew—pass a Washington to the portly shopkeep: the ticket to his thirty minutes in heaven with the girls.

It seemed too good to be true. It had to be. And by the look on the clerk's face, probably it was.

"—so tell him to get out," he heard Brandon say.

"We told you we were gonna—"

"I don't give a shit, kid. Justin already paid, so kick bricks and wait your turn. My manager doesn't like y'all slinking around in here."

Justin, Colin shuddered. *Oh no…*

Tony slammed his nail polished fists onto the checkout booth. "Fuck this," he said, and barged his way to the back of the store.

Brandon whipped his devil's grin at the clerk and followed.

"Aw, shit," Cara cackled. "It's fucking on!" She raced into Bazookas and made for the dressing room.

"Fight, fight, fight," Andrea chanted, dragging Colin through the entry by his chained jeans, and they hop-skipped like corn sack racers past a spinning shelf of lurid greeting cards. He banged his knee into a stack of phallic chia pets, she kicked them away with her enormous rubber soles. Broken terracotta and muffled cardboard.

"Stop," the clerk cried out. "You guys are gonna get me canned!"

Colin and Andrea made it to the changing room just as Tony jerked open the red curtains. Sitting on a wooden stool within was the form of Colin's most feared classmate. Not just a bully, no, a high-school terrorist known to beat kids blue by the backside of his Dad's revolver for chump change. He of tanned skin stark against a flimsy off-white sweatsuit and bright Nike dunks. Pierced eyebrows, studded tongue. The smell of Abercrombie cologne and seed-choked cannabis.

"Close the curtain, you fuckin' freaks," Justin said. An open backpack sat near his thong strapped feet and a collection of snack sized plastic bags filled with purple pills sat on his lap. The pills were pressed with ying-yang symbols and rudimentary smiley-faces. "You buying or leaving?"

"This room's already booked," Brandon said with his chin resting on Tony's shoulder. "Get your shit and leave."

"What'd you say?"

"He said *get the fuck out*," Tony reached into clapboard enclosure, grabbed the backpack, and tossed it down an aisle. "We ain't playing around, you jock-itch motherfucker."

Justin stood tall, teeming with I-got-held-back-a-grade muscles and pre-adulthood rage. The drug baggies clattered to the floor. His hand dipped into the milky waistband of his joggers and flashed the stubby leather handle of a gun. "Who's playing?"

Cara lurched behind Brandon and Tony. She pushed the boys into the changing room and shouted with glee. "Get his shooter," she said, "bust him one in the nuts!"

Andrea jumped up and down in a fit of excitement. Her straps jangled as Colin ducked down to the floor. Prone as a board, he covered his head with both palms. Sweat spread across his trench coat and prayers for peace littered his tongue.

"Teach you to pull a fucking gun on me." Tony frothed at the mouth and wrapped his bicep around Justin's neck.

Brandon reached for the revolver but was felled by a wild, sandaled kick. He dropped to the ground heavily. From his new view, Brandon glanced at Colin—still limp and whimpering—with radioactive disgust. "Get up, you little worm," he said.

"Aw, *shit*," The Bazookas cashier stood back from the group. He brandished a cold lava lamp bottle, and shook it at the brawling teens. "Everybody, cool out!"

Tony managed a full headlock and hauled the violet-faced Justin out into the store. Every time the older boy tried to grab the gun, Tony pulled a sharp knee up into his groin with a snap. Over and over, the sack was mashed as Justin gagged and wheezed.

Brandon got himself up off the floor and returned a devastating kick to Justin's bread-basket. He laughed and did it again, then helped Tony drag him through the store.

Cara trailed them as close as she could manage. She hopped back and forth between the whirling boys for a better look at the action. Her lips smacked in rabid excitement and her bell-bottoms rippled so that the faux flames stitched upon them danced with life.

Andrea was forced to pull Colin down the aisles by the hem of his gigantic pant leg. In her haste to see bloodshed, her quaking, sharp nailed fingers could not undo the binding links that tethered them together. She cursed him for his cowardice, and chortled with disgust at the stream of urine he left in their wake.

Colin closed himself off. Felt nothing. Lost at sea, far beneath the ebon waves.

Outside Bazookas, full pandemonium ensued. Fists were thrown, eyes were blacked, and teeth loosed in their youthful moorings. Painted claws raked and tore. Sweaty backs were hunched and daring slurs were cast. Bedazzled shoppers stared on with hunger. Concerned citizens shepherded away their disaffected brood.

The revolver, at last, came free from the waistband. It bounced on tile, end over end, clanked and clacked, barrel cartwheeling with reckless aim.

Colin chanced a look, turned his head from where he lay, and watched the gun slide past him. He saw a ratty sneaker come down on top to cease its random path; a hairy arm that stooped to clutch its handle. A stack of pamphlets emblazoned with the crucifix drifted all around.

Bearded face. Drunken glare. Heart of a bleeding zealot.

Colin flipped over on his side.

Jeb Jacobs held out the revolver. "In the name of Jesus," he said. "Behold!"

Justin's chest caved in. A jarring pop that damned all ears. Then, the ringing death of flabbergasted eardrums. An instant explosion of bone and blood, one millisecond of fire and ash. The teen delinquent crumpled, gasped like a fish on dry land.

Tony fell back and slammed his tailbone on the floor. Brandon took hard, sucking breaths. Cara ran away, tucked herself into another store. Andrea kicked free from her aluminum chains and she too disappeared. Colin lay still and watched Justin bleed to death.

"See what happens when the wicked meet the hand of God," Jeb Jacobs said. He held out his arms, gun cocked to one side, and shouted: "Begone, sinner! May thou suckle for an eternity at Satan's curdled teat."

A pool of liquid red leaked from the dead boy's body and circled him. At Jeb Johnson's proclamation, the blood began to sizzle as if spoken to. It beaded and shook like water to a skillet, then cracked and broke open. Blue flames leapt from the boiling ichor and gnarled, three-fingered hands breached the molten crust. The ghoulish hands took hold of Justin and quickly, deliberately, ripped him into small pieces. Like toddler hands on soft bread, the alien fingers took the teen apart until the smaller and smaller pieces became nothing at all. The hands dipped beneath the azure fire and vanished. The charred circle of blackened life crackled like desert earth and was blown away by strange winds.

Nothing was left. Not a crumb. No hellfire remnants or clues of damnation.

"Now," Jeb Jacobs said, "Hear me..."

*

"My name is Jebediah Brady Jacobs. Y'all know who I am. You know what I done. You seen me at my worst—my most *sinful*. And because of who I was before the Lord come to me, I know none of y'all will believe what I got to say.

"So I reckon I'll have to show you.

"See, the Lord God has set me on a mission to save each and every one of your souls. No matter what you done, He loves you. God *wants* to forgive. He don't want none of you to wind up in the icy fires of Hades. He wants to help you atone for your sins. Just like he done for me.

"God has given me His greatest gift: He has sat me upon one of his mighty Thrones. We can get you straight, send you to the gates of peace and love. But if you ain't got right with Him before you meet the reaper, well, there ain't nothing that can save you from Satan his-own-self.

"Now see the truth."

Jeb Jacobs popped open his mouth, placed the muzzle inside. He tasted the blood of Christ and savored the rich flavor, just for a moment. His finger flexed upon the trigger.

And all was light.

*

The head of Jeb Jacobs exploded, upwards and out. Skull fragments splintered into high velocity shrapnel and pierced the skin of slack-jawed onlookers. A crimson fountain erupted in splendorous release, spraying the small crowd with hot, gummy spurts.

Brandon and Tony were speechless and wet; pockmarked with bone studs like flesh bruising birdshot.

Colin was drenched. Fouled and reeking by way of an assortment of bodily fluids; his trenchcoat and jeans, filthy with liquids both of his own making and those expelled by the recently deceased. He watched Jeb Jacobs take small, stuttering steps.

Most of the man's head was gone—only the bottom half of his whiskered jaw remained. The tongue swayed across yellowish bottom teeth, licked nervously at the new vacancy.

There came from aloft, a high and baleful sound that seemed to drift on the ether; it was akin to the hollow tones of the mall's speaker system, yet one could still hear the standard ambient tune on a monotonous loop throughout the building. The sound grew louder and soon drowned out the elevator music and screaming patrons.

The noise reminded Colin of the quarter semester he endured in the school's marching band. Back when using his guitar skills for a scholarship credit had seemed like a good idea. That was before Justin and his goon squad pulled him under the bleachers to steal his Game Boy…Before Justin died and got sent to Hell with his old man's gun by a Bible thumping maniac.

Colin had little time or energy to ponder the familiar, bleating noise: *Why, God, why,* he wondered, *why is Jeb Jacobs still standing?*

The corpse indeed still walked, and—as the sound intensified—a white hot jolt of violent force blasted from the gurgling waste of Jeb Jacobs' neck. Like a spotlight was chambered in his belly, a brilliant ivory glare seeped from his pores and cast out from his fingertips. The tube of light that extended where his head once sat pulsed with extraordinary hues: flittering gold, and icy blue silver—fragments of candy floss pink, the suggestion of shadowy pigments perhaps unfit for human eyes.

Tony got up from where he fell. He slipped on a

stray gout of blood, and regained himself. On shaky legs—his shrieking assbone—he hobbled over to Brandon and shielded his face from the light.

Brandon stared into the beam with dazed intensity. Unable to look away, drawn like a pale moth. "I can see," he said. "I see it."

Tony grabbed his oldest friend by the shoulders. "Come on, man," he said. "This ain't right. We got to—"

"*Lo!*" The word was clear. A brash, unforgiving voice that filled the minds of all who basked in the glorious light. "*Behold*," it said, and it was the command of a cyclopean mouth from beyond the veil of reality; a word sent down from an opal throne; the proclative oration of cosmic supremacy.

The tube of light which juttered from Jeb Jacobs' neck shortened, then widened. It broke in two, like a Lazer Dome light show, and each end curved outward to reveal a voided center. The beams connected, formed a circle, and another appeared in the radial blackout. With the swishing of wings, the two circles of light began to revolve around each other. Slowly, at first, then gaininged in speed. In their delicate movements, the whirling lights revealed themselves as thick bands, like rings, and along their smooth curves, dreadful eyeballs were set like precious stones. The alien eyes twitched and rolled with pupils that followed scrambling shoppers to fixate on them and their children.

A wide array of eyes on the innermost ring fell suddenly upon Colin—the majority, in fact, though it was difficult to discern as the eyes seemed endless in number.

Colin did not dare to move. He instead muttered incessant prayers as Jeb Jacobs' feet lifted from the floor and swiftly hovered towards him. The whirling light of winking eyes and golden rings bore down from above as if pulling the corpse by a string.

The thing was upon him and the boy looked at it and knew that it was an angel. He could see a kingdom beyond the black hole between each band, and in the undulating aurora borealis dancing along the halo horizon, Colin saw his Grandfather. He wrapped the leather duster around himself and took a deep breath; beyond the blood and piss and sweat and sad-little-boy, Colin could still smell him: the best friend he ever had.

You're a good kid, his Grandfather would have said.

The angel forced the hand of Jeb Jacobs to point a finger at the cowering child. A ray of stunning shine emitted from beneath the nail and Colin was set aglow.

Tony had Brandon in a chokehold similar to the one he used on the dead dealer no more than six minutes prior. *Maybe less*, he thought. Everything happened so quickly, but then again, it was hard to focus on the passing of time while an armed Jesus Freak gave a sermon outside the novelty shop. "We got to get out of here, man!"

"It's—it's—what—" Brandon stammered. His corneas held reflective glare; two brass shields in the sun. "What's it doing to him?"

Tony turned and saw the floating corpse rise above Colin like a cursed wasp. The boy shone as bright as the face of a morning pond. The thing-that-was-Jeb-Jacobs seemed to lift him by the crook of its finger, and Colin's limp form flew up into the air.

"I'm alright, guys," he called down to his friends from on high. "It's okay now. I'll be seeing my Grandpa soon, can you believe it?" His voice rang true with hopeful bliss. "I'm going home."

The angel twisted the hand of Jeb Jacobs and a man-sized cross materialized behind the skybound teen. Colin's arms wrenched back on either side of the crucifix and his feet clapped together, stiff and straight.

Tony jumped, startled by the impossible conjuring. He let go of Brandon, watched in awe. "What the fuck?"

The angel spread the fingers, and so too appeared three cruel nails. The spikes drifted through nothing and formed an inverted triangle around the boy on his cross. A sizable length of thorned vine came down from the sky, ate its tail by unseen forces, and cinched itself to Colin's skull like a headband. The nails took aim and dove into his feet and hands with a crunch.

Colin started to scream, but the sound that had filled his brain when the angel first appeared now returned. *A trumpet*, he thought, *a horn to welcome me into his loving—*

The crucified kid imploded. Evaporated. Only a dull echo remained, like the strum of a massive harp. Vague glitter and oddly shaped embers swayed lazily above and fanned around the rafters.

Colin was gone.

"Jesus Titty-Fuckin' Christ," Tony said.

Brandon, shaken from his stupor, wheeled on him. "Quiet," he said. "Thou shalt not take the Lord's name—"

The angel turned to them, and the corpse began to move. It drifted with nauseating speed and soon hung before Brandon. Again, the dead man's hand was lifted like a marionette to point down at him.

Wheels of brilliance, eyes of holy terror.

Tony leapt to one side as a bolt shot out from Jeb Jacobs' fingertips. The light enveloped Brandon until he burned like yellow coal.

"Oh, God," Brandon moaned. "It hurts."

Tony meant to run and hide but could not look away from his glowing compadre. Brandon writhed on the tile beside him, slapped his palms and kicked his legs. His back arched, then buckled. Blood squelched from underneath him and lapped at Tony's boots.

"I'm so sorry I was bad," Brandon said. "Please, forgive me!"

Tony heard a sickening pop. It reminded him of animal bones being bashed in with the hammer he had unearthed at a construction site near his childhood apartment; like windshields he destroyed by chucking boulders at vacant cars beneath lakeside bluffs.

More blood gushed across the floor from under

Brandon's back. He sat up suddenly—wrenched forward as if pushed—and two sets of wings unfolded. The wings flexed to shake off their blood clotted feathers, and like the down of swans, the great wings were ivory beneath the gore and human waste from which they emerged. As the wings pumped, the teen rose from the floor and hovered beside the angel.

"Am I redeemed?" Brandon asked between sucking sobs. "Can I sit beside him?"

The trumpet sounded and the wings beat faster. Brandon rose higher and higher; he skyrocketed up towards a windowed roof and disappeared with a snap before reaching the glass.

Two bone-white feathers dropped from the rafters. Tony watched them fall and could not decide whether to shout or get as far away as his legs would carry him. The feathers flipped end over end with graceful leisure, then they too vanished, as had his oldest friend.

The angel turned to Tony and he stared back at its many roving eyes with seething hate for each and every one of them.

"Die, you motherfucker!"

Cara appeared behind the angel, revolver in her

hands. The muzzle flared and four shots rang out. Where punctured, the corpse of Jeb Jacobs oozed slow, unsavory blood. Andrea sprouted up beside her and lashed her pant-chains like a whip.

The angel did not turn its puppet body to meet them, and instead forced the arms to bend backwards with ease. On grinding tendons and broken bones, the dead man's fingers waggled their beams of light upon the girls.

Tony finally ran. His boots slapped hard on the floor and he shoved any remaining rubberneckers and panic-stricken families out of his way. Shouts and shrieks of horror followed him. He felt a warmth at his back, and could sense brightness at the edges of his vision.

"God, help us," he heard Cara shout beneath the buzzing of one billion phantom locusts.

"In His name," Andrea cried, and the roar of roiling waves crashed through the halls.

The fire at Tony's back intensified. His skin blistered beneath his favorite shirt and he wondered if he was on fire. He stopped, panting, and doubled over. With hand to belly, the teenager heaved, and pink vomit descended from his throat.

"Shit," he said.

When Tony regained himself, he removed the palm from his stomach to wipe at his mouth and found that it was full of blood.

He was especially proud of his bottle-toss-earned Slipknot tee because his favorite band member was featured so prominently. It pained him to see a wide bullet hole through the masked axe-slayer's head; more so to watch a garish trickle of green bile dribble down to his waist.

His skin raged like an Autumn bon, felt fit to drip from his bones. He tasted char in his spit; frost and smoke rattled his lungs. Hellfire lapped at his swollen feet and Tony knew the Devil would come for him soon.

With stinging eyes, he looked away from his ventilated gut. He found himself standing in the entrance of World of Wonders, and the sword spoke his name.

*

The angel floated through the Mall and saved the streaming sinners in its wake. Holy bolts shot out from the corpse of Jeb Jacobs with seemingly wild abandon, yet each and every ray found its mark.

Glowing bodies were shuttled into the air to twist and writhe. Ribs were gouged by the apparitions of Roman spears. Flesh was peeled from backs by barbed lashes and invisible hands. Those touched by the light begged mercy until God's forgiveness launched them into His heavenly Kingdom.

The unfortunate few who were merely trampled by their brethren burned in rings of Hellfire. No salvation for those not baptized in His majestic warmth. Darkness and pain. Damnation, eternal.

Near the food-court, the angel's many rolling eyes lighted upon a pack of elderly men and women in walking shoes and sweats. The wheels of splendor turned with ferocious speed. Braying trumpets blared their gospel and the luminosity of divine grandeur filled the halls.

"Jesus wept," an old man cried as the angel swayed in front of them.

"*Lo*," the angel said. "*Be*—"

"Ave Satanas!"

A growling voice cut through the choral tones in rapturous gravel and a throat of smoke. The righteous trumpets dissolved beneath its mighty roar. The voice sent out vibrations that shook the mall-walkers in their jumpsuits and rattled the precious ores welded to their teeth.

The angel wheeled with eyes sliding to and fro. Its rings churned and the headless corpse of Jeb Jacobs twitched in a macabre gesture of surprise.

A shadow fell across the angel and its vessel.

"Ave Domini Inferi," the rumbling voice spoke again.

From above, high among the raftered ceiling, a crimson form descended. Wrapped in black clouds, it came down with the flexing wings of a monstrous bat and landed on thick, cloven hooves. Three horns protruded from its red skull like the crown of wicked kings, and a forked tongue skimmed its ruby lips. Naked save a bulge of masculine goat hair upon its loins, the molten flesh ruffled with impossible muscle.

The huddled elderly walkers held each other and trembled in fear. The old man looked back and forth between the angel and the hellish beast that stood before it. "What in God's name—?"

The demon stepped to the angel, and in one clawed fist, a sword was held aloft. Curved blade, handle of red, freed from its slumber in the mortal realm. A World of Wonders price-tag dangled with obscenity from the knuckle-brace handle. The demon's black eyes twinkled, engorged and oddly humored. Teeth of a subaquatic predator; round red face of a delinquent cherub.

"You fucked up my best shirt," the Tony-demon said. The sound of his new voice sent a thrilling gust of pleasure down his barbed spine. He tasted the angel's fear on his snake-tongue. "I walk about as a roaring lion," he gnashed, "seeking to devour."

The angel jerked the hands of Jeb Jacobs and twin volts of glory unleashed from the fingers. Light erupted and was soon enveloped by the inky storm billowing about the Tony-demon. The angel tried to strike again and again on snapping wrists and rigor mortis limbs. Over and over the holy light was cast, but could not penetrate the unholy pall.

The Tony-demon laughed. He flipped out the sword in one deft swoop and its blade came to roost in the angel's center ring. "Tell God to eat shit," he said, and the angel flared in a drizzle of spark and bombastic rays. It burst like a Black Cat bottle rocket, zipped upwards and away. The trumpet ceased and the mall soundtrack resumed its loop of inoffensive ambience.

The angel was gone. Gone as if it had never come to earth. As if it never was.

"Oh, Jesus, *thank you*," the elderly mall-walker

said. He stood up from the floor and cast uneasy eyes of gratitude at the sword-wielding behemoth. "I don't know what you are, Sonny, but we are so—"

"Who am I?" The Tony-demon asked. He raised one crooked eyebrow and smirked. "I am *many*," he answered. "And you—"

The old man gulped. He retreated to his blue-haired commune and planted his bony seat back to tile. The elderly walkers held each other with thin, shaking arms.

"—*you* are all mine." The Tony-demon raised his cruel sword and fell upon them. "I been waiting for this."

OUT OF HAND
JON STEFFENS

Kevin's dad parked his black Chevy Silverado in front of the modest home on Eastbrook Drive. A yellow porch light illuminated the dingy brown front door and cracked porch. Darkness obscured the home's peeling white paint and sagging soffit. The thumping bass of "Pussy" by Lords of Acid rattled the cloudy front window. Kevin opened the door to step from the truck when his old man's voice made him pause.

"Hey bud, you sure you're good to get a ride home?"

"Yeah, dad," Kevin did his best to not appear annoyed. "Brad is supposed to show up tonight. I'll ride with him."

"Okay, son. Be careful. Call home if you need anything."

The six-foot teenager stepped from the truck. Kevin's father sped off, AC/DC's "Whole Lotta Rosie" blasting from the pickup's stereo loud enough the dual exhaust couldn't drown it out.

Kevin modeled his appearance after his jock-goth idols Peter Steele and Glenn Danzig. With his shaggy, dyed-black hair parted in the middle, leather motorcycle jacket, Cradle of Filth t-shirt, black Dickies jeans, and physique like a chubby linebacker who spent the entirety of his workouts doing bench presses and bicep curls, the husky man-sized child looked far more like the bully in a teen sitcom than his favorite beefy, brooding rock stars.

The soles of his army surplus combat boots echoed off the uneven pavement as he strode toward the house. Kevin's posture was straight, his head held high and his chest out. He hoped to appear confident, though he was anything but. This would be Kevin's first time hanging out with his girlfriend Michelle without his parents around. They never spent time at Michelle's place. Her mom was a drug addict who lived in the shitty apartments by the meth motel.

After a few unanswered knocks, Kevin let

himself in. The living room was bathed in black light. A choking mix of smoke from cloves, weed, and tobacco hung in the air. Someone changed the CD in the stereo. Kevin was relieved the bumping Belgian sex-techno had been replaced by the aggressive rumble of some industrial metal band he couldn't recognize.

Scanning the room for a familiar face, Kevin saw his friend Matt. With Kevin's CD collection made up of mostly goth, punk, and black metal, he often judged the music tastes of his schoolmates as if he were the Lord of the Underground. Matt made Kevin seem like a pop-radio-listening jock. The music the skinny, bespectacled high-school junior enjoyed was truly out there –a weirdo bouquet of Japanese harsh noise, lo-fi indie rock, occult-inspired freeform jazz, and a host of other oddities. Kevin made his way through the group of mall-goths and mean-mugging trailer park metal kids, clapping Matt on the shoulder.

"Hey man, what's up?" Kevin smirked.

"Hey Kev," Matt's eyes looked past him. "This music sucks. Just here to see if Joey has any acid."

"Oh, cool. Haha," Kevin laughed awkwardly. Wile no stranger to imbibing copious amounts of cheap whiskey and beer, he was terrified of drugs. His dad smoked weed, and Kevin was pretty sure he did coke with the thugs who stopped by for drinks on weekends. Kevin wasn't about it, though. Alcohol was enough for him. "You see Michelle around?"

"Nah, man. I got here just before you walked in. Joey!" Matt walked toward a tall, thin kid wearing a fishnet shirt, black fingernail polish, and eyeliner.

Kevin looked around once more for any recognizable faces before going down through a door into the kitchen. Mindy greeted him, smiling. He'd never admit it to Michelle, but Kevin had a major crush on Mindy before being introduced to his girlfriend by their mutual friend Amy.

Mindy was tall, had a great body, and a pretty face. She wore fishnets under black cutoff jean shorts, a black t-shirt with Bela Lugosi's ghoulish visage displayed across the front, and black lipstick. Her head was mostly shaved down to a buzzcut minus her bands, which were dyed green. Most importantly to Kevin, she liked good music. Mostly.

"Hi Kev," her pleasant smile lit up the dark room. "Thanks for coming over! Jello shot?"

"Uh, yes please," Though he could have passed for nearly 30, the fifteen-year-old's deep voice cracked. She handed him two, one red, the other green. He downed both, and his throat burned. "What's in these?" he asked, stifling a cough.

"Everclear!" She smiled. "Want another one?"

"No thanks," Kevin shook his head. "Do you have any beer?"

"Right here" Tara reached her hand over his shoulder, offering a Miller High Life.

"Sweet!" Kevin's eyes lit up as he grabbed the cold gold-and-red can. "Have you guys seen Michelle?"

Tara and Mindy shot each other a look so quickly Keven didn't pick up on it. "She said she'll be here in an hour or so." Tara smiled at him. "Let's go get you a buzz in the meantime!" The two girls led Kevin to the back porch. An abrasive hardcore song blared a tinny buzz from the worn-out speakers of an old jambox. Outside is where the cool punk and goth kids were sharing swigs from a bottle of Jack Daniels. No Manson-worshipping mall goths or kids in Korn t-shirts. These outsiders were all into old-school 80s goth rock or underground street punk.

"This is more like it!" Kevin lowered himself into a lawn chair. Mindy sat in his lap while Tara fed him a steady stream of beers. Kevin didn't question his pampering.

Things played out much the same for the following hour or so. Everyone had slipped into a warm drunken haze. Mindy playfully kissed his ear while teenagers sat around trying to sound important to each other. Kevin knew he should have asked Mindy to stop, but he was having far too much fun. After five beers, Kevin needed to relieve himself. He stood up, his legs a bit wobbly. Mindy told him he could piss on the side of the house, then went back to chatting with Tara as two other girls, Rachel and Keri, stepped onto the back porch. To the delight of everyone, they brought a freshly packed pipe and a bottle of vodka. Kevin stumbled to the side of the house, where three older-looking kids high on meth were talking about nothing at a hundred miles an hour. *Shit*, he thought to himself. Neither Mindy, Tara, nor anyone else noticed Kevin slip through the back door into the kitchen.

The smoke was heavier inside now. Kevin hated it even more than he hated crowded kitchens. Making his way through the group of high school outcasts, Kevin exited the kitchen into a sparsely packed living room. Two kids clad in Pantera shirts took turns taking pulls from a fifth of cheap whiskey in the corner. Joey sat on the couch watching *The Doom Generation* on VHS, flanked by two girls Kevin had never seen before. One was in a white tank top while the other sported a black Korn tee. Both wore baggy JNCOs. The acid must have kicked in, as they stared unblinking at the silent television screen while the sounds of Ministry's "N.W.O." shook the walls from the CD deck.

Kevin turned right into the hallway, the urge to piss still nagging his bladder. He opened the first door and was hit by the scent of patchouli. Posters and pinups of The Cramps, Nine Inch Nails, Marilyn Manson, Type O Negative, Bauhaus, and Deadsy crowded the walls. A black fleece blanket was draped across the full-size bed. A lava lamp on the dresser cast a faint purple glow across the walls. Mindy's room.

The next door Kevin opened ruined the party for all in attendance. Brian Rutherford –local dirtbag and twenty-two-year-old drug dealer who hung around high school parties—was seated on an old plaid loveseat. Leaned back with his eyes closed and his jeans unzipped, his right hand rested on Michelle's head as it bobbed up and down on Brian's crotch. The sloppy, wet slurping sounds that filled the room turned Kevin's stomach.

"What the absolute *fuck*?" Kevin's voice boomed. The house suddenly seemed as quiet as midnight in a library.

Michelle turned her head, a terrified look on her face. Her shoulder-length black hair was a tousled mess. A single string of drool ran from Michelle's bottom lip to the head of Brian's cock. In an instant, Brian roughly shoved Michelle aside, the back of her head slamming into the wood-paneled wall. Trying to stand, Brian reached into his pocket to pull out the small folding knife he kept on himself, but with a speed that seemed too quick for his size, Kevin's right fist smashed into Brian's nose, breaking it. Blood spattered both their faces and gushed over Brian's lips and chin. Dazed, Brian fell back onto the couch. The knife was in his hand. Kevin wasn't sure how he'd opened the blade so quickly.

"Motherfucker! You ain't cutting shit!" Kevin screamed as he straddled Brian, the drug dealer's limp dick still out of his pants. Kevin's fists rained down on Brain's already battered face. Blows cracked into his jaw, cheek, eyes, and forehead until Kevin's knuckles were bloodied. Michelle screamed for Kevin to stop. If he heard her, he ignored her sobbing pleas. Brian shakily raised the knife toward Kevin, who wrenched it from the battered man's hand. Kevin stood and jammed the knife into Brian's groin repeatedly. Wounds opened on his penis, scrotum, and pubic mound. Finally, Kevin pushed the blade deep enough into Brian's crotch hot blood ran over his hand. His voice a shrill wail, Brian screamed through broken teeth before passing out.

Tara and Mindy rushed into the room. Wrapping a blanket around Michelle, they led their sobbing friend from the room. The gathered crowd stared cautiously at Kevin, like he was a crazed animal. Brian lay on the ruined couch in a bloody heap. Though his face was a nearly unrecognizable mess of swollen flesh, broken bone, and blood, he was breathing. After a few deep breaths to steady himself, Kevin left the room to look for Michelle. The kids parted quickly to let him through.

Kevin stepped into the backyard. A handful of party goers had left, but most remained. Aside from the girls quietly consoling Michelle, all were silent. No one called the cops. Everyone had been drinking and partaking of several other substances all night, and the only adult at the residence was the brutalized drug dealer. A police presence was the last thing anyone wanted. Tara stepped toward Kevin as he approached.

"You have to leave, Kev. What the fuck is wrong with you?"

"Let me talk to Michelle," Kevin said, and pushed past Tara.

"Get the fuck out of here!" Michelle screamed at

Kevin through her tears.

"Fuck that." Kevin sounded cold. "I thought you were my girlfriend?"

"We hung out twice!" Michelle sobbed. "Every time I tried to touch you, you acted scared! I figured you didn't want me! At least Brian knows what he wants!"

Kevin's face turned red at the mention of his inexperience. Michelle was his first girlfriend. He really had no clue how to act when they were alone. He thought he showed her plenty of affection, but it wasn't what she needed from him. "Fuck that piece of shit," Kevin said defiantly. "He's a scumbag drug dealer! Like he gives a shit about you or anyone else!"

"Fuck you, Kevin! If you won't leave, I will!" She got up, still wrapped only in a gray blanket, and strode toward the door leading into the kitchen. Kevin started to follow.

"Kev," Mindy pleaded, "Leave her alone. Give her some space."

Ignoring her, Kevin went inside. Michelle was

standing in the empty living room, gulping from a bottle of cheap vodka. The TV showed only static. The stereo was silent. Kevin approached from behind her and lightly grasped her arm.

"Don't touch me, you fucking psycho!" Michelle wrenched her arm from his grasp and went for the front door.

"Michelle, please," Kevin desperately tried to smooth things over. The large fifteen-year-old didn't know what love was, but he thought he felt it for her. Though Kevin had brutally assaulted someone down the hall, all he could think about was trying to fix the situation with Michelle. He quickly strode after her.

"Leave me alone! Asshole!" She turned and spat at Kevin as he closed the gap between them. Crying, she broke into a run toward the street.

"Michelle! Stop!" Kevin cried as he reached for her, but it was too late.

The moment Michelle stepped into the street a tow truck plowed into the slight girl, her body instantly destroyed in a hail of gore. Blood and chunks of viscera coated Kevin and the hood of a champagne-colored Honda to his right. Kevin fell to a seated position and screamed. His bladder failed, warm piss soaking his pants. Michelle's top half came to rest two feet from Kevin's right boot, her remaining eye staring at Kevin lifelessly.

About the Authors

Sam Richard is the author of *Grief Rituals*, *Sabbath of the Fox-Devils*, and the award-winning *To Wallow in Ash & Other Sorrows*. He has edited ten anthologies, including the cult hits *Profane Sorcery* and *The New Flesh*, and his short fiction has appeared in over forty publications. Widowed in 2017, he slowly rots in Minneapolis where he runs Weirdpunk Books. You can stalk him @SammyTotep across socials or at weirdpunkbooks.com

Xavier Garcia is a writer/editor from Toronto, Canada. His short fiction has appeared in various magazines and anthologies published by Fugitives & Futurists, Cold Signal, hex, Apocalypse Confidential, Cursed Morsels, Filthy Loot, and others. You can find him walking the nightmare corpse-city of R'lyeh, or at twitter.com/xavier_agarcia.

Matthew Mitchell is a fiction and comics writer from the Ozarks. His debut novella *Chaindevils* received the Literary Nasties Award, and his short fiction has been published in various anthologies such as the award-winning *Void Haus*. Matthew's comics have appeared in Heavy Metal Magazine and he is co-editor of the Horrorium comics anthology.

Jon Steffens is one of four people in the world who still listens to Deadsy. He lives in shame of this fact near Fort Worth, Texas

FILTHY LOOT is an independent press, based out of Ames, IA. Focused on misfit fictions and odd other ideas — we publish books, zines and assorted miscellany in both open and limited edition formats.

- ☐ *a beginner's guide to extreme horror* by Jon Steffens & Ira Rat
- ☐ *Gone to Seed* by Justin Lutz
- ☐ *Hairs* by Ira Rat
- ☐ *Hollow Coin* by S.T. Cartledge
- ☐ *My Mind is Not a Billboard//What's Your Favorite TV Show?* by Sam Pink
- ☐ *Pacifier* by Ira Rat
- ☐ *Participation Trophy* by Ira Rat
- ☐ *Shagging the Boss* by Rebecca Rowland
- ☐ *The Doom that Came To Mellonville* by Madison McSweeny
- ☐ *The God in the Hills and Other Horrors* by Jon Steffens
- ☐ *The God in the Hills 2: Abhorent Flesh* by Jon Steffens
- ☐ *The Vine that Ate the Starlet* by Madeleine Swann
- ☐ *Wax and Wane* by Saoirse Ní Chiaragáin

Anthologies
- ☐ *Dirt in the Sky* (Anthology)
- ☐ *Fucked Up Stories to Read in the Daytime* (Anthology)
- ☐ *Isolation is Safety* (Anthology)
- ☐ *LAZERMALL* (Anthology)
- ☐ *Soft Ceremonies* (Anthology)
- ☐ *Teenage Grave* (Anthology)
- ☐ *Teenage Grave 2* (Anthology)

www.ingramcontent.com/pod-product-compliance
Lightning Source LLC
LaVergne TN
LVHW092056060526
838201LV00047B/1414